This book
belongs to

....

Puddle's Fan Pages

Here's what other children have to say about their favourite puppy and his third adventure!

"This is such an exciting story. I really liked that they went to a ballet and thought it was good that when they arrived they thought they were in a forest but were on the stage. Puddle is very funny." Ava, age 7

"It was fantastic. I liked it being set in the theatre and my favourite bit was when they went to the props room and played with the Cinderella coach." Caitlin, age 6

"I would like to do dancing like Ruby and have ballet shoes." Lucina, age 5

"This book was really good. I liked the ballet. Puddle is very cute but he is quite naughty sometimes!" Saara, age 6

"I really liked this book. It was great to meet Puddle and Ruby and Harry again." Madeleine, age 5

"My favourite bit was at the end, when everyone was throwing roses, because they were all smiling and I like the picture." Kyla, age 6

"I like the bit when Puddle dances." Jena, age 3

Ballet Show Mischief

Other books about
Puddle the Naughtiest Puppy:
Magic Carpet Ride
Toyshop Trouble
Rainforest Hide and Seek

Puddle
the naughtiest puppy

Ballet Show Mischief

by Hayley Daze
illustrated by Livia Coloji
cover illustrated by Paul Hardman

A catalogue record for this book is available from the British Library

Published by Ladybird Books Ltd MMX
A Penguin Company
Penguin Books Ltd., 80 Strand, London WC2R 0RL, UK
Penguin Books Australia Ltd., Camberwell, Victoria, Australia
Penguin Group (NZ) 67 Apollo Drive, Rosedale,
North Shore 0632, New Zealand

1 3 5 7 9 10 8 6 4 2
Series created by Working Partners Limited, London WC1X 9HH
Text and illustrations © Working Partners Ltd MMX

Special thanks to Mo O'Hara

ISBN: 978-1-40930-329-9
Printed in England

Mixed Sources

Product group from well-managed
forests and other controlled sources
www.fsc.org   Cert no. SA-COC-001592
© 1996 Forest Stewardship Council

FSC

To my mom and dad
for all their love and support

When clouds fill the sky and rain starts to fall,
Ruby and Harry are not sad at all.
They know that when puddles appear on the ground,
A magical puppy will soon be around!

Puddle's his name, and he's the one
Who can lead you to worlds of adventure and fun!
He may be quite naughty, but he's clever too,
So come follow Puddle – he's waiting for you!

A present from Puddle:

Look out for the special code at the back of the book to
get extra-special games and loads of free stuff at Puddle's
website! Come and play at www.puddlethepuppy.com

Contents

Chapter One
On with the Show

"Ladies and gentlemen, the show
is about to begin!" Ruby shouted
from behind the plush red bedspread
hanging across Grandad's lounge.
She closed her eyes for a moment and
imagined a huge theatre filled with
people, calling her name.

"Ruby! Ruby!"

She waved to her imaginary fans,

until she realized they sounded like
her cousin Harry.

"Ruby! Ruby, can you hear me?
What are you doing back there?"
he asked.

"It's a surprise." She giggled,
and peeked around the bedspread.
"Ready?"

"Um, sorry, Ruby, I've got to finish
this maze," Harry said, pushing his
glasses back in place and burying
his nose in a puzzle book.

Never mind, Ruby thought as she ducked back behind the curtain, *the show must go on.* She took a big breath and tugged on her plaits for luck. Her stomach felt as if it was being tickled by fairy wings. She pulled back her pretend curtain.

"Welcome to Ruby's Enchanted Ballet," she said, holding the edges of her wrinkly tutu and curtsying like she'd seen real dancers do. The wall behind Ruby was covered with drawings of rainbows, castles, mountains and forests. Ruby had coloured them all in herself, on separate sheets of paper, and taped them together.

She twirled around on her tiptoes
with her arms high above her head.
But her socks were slippery. Her legs
slid in opposite directions, causing
Ruby to accidentally do the splits.
"Ta da!" she sang, with her arms
outstretched, turning the splits into a
part of her dance routine.

"So that's what you've been working on all morning," Harry said, and closed his puzzle book.

Ruby pushed the 'play' button on Grandad's CD player and soft violin music filled the air. "Now watch me do a spinning top," she said, holding out her tutu and twirling to the music.

"Those are called pirouettes,"
Harry corrected her, "but I think
you hold your arms out like this."
He got up from his chair and spun
round on his toes
with his arms
curved in front
of him, using
them
to help
him whirl
round.
"Woah, that
really makes
you dizzy,"
he said, sitting
down again.

"And this is my graceful swan," Ruby said. She balanced on one foot and stuck out her arms like wings.

"The real name for that is an arabesque," Harry said.

"I like my name better," Ruby replied, still on one foot. "How come you know so much about ballet?"

"My parents love watching ballet at the theatre, and sometimes they make me go too," Harry said.

Just then the wind blew the front
door open with a *BANG!* Ruby's
pictures were whipped from the wall.
They swirled around the living room
and finally fluttered to the floor.
A puppy dashed on to Ruby's stage
and shook himself, spraying water
everywhere.

"Puddle!" shouted Ruby, twirling on her toes in delight.

Every time it rained, Puddle the naughty little puppy appeared and swept Ruby and Harry off on a magical adventure.

"Now that's what I call an entrance," Harry said with a laugh.

Puddle tugged at the curtain until it was closed.

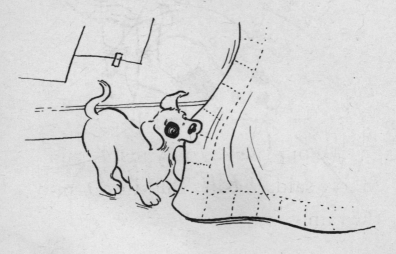

"I guess that means my show is over," Ruby said, taking a sweeping bow.

"But our fun has only just begun!" Harry said, chasing Puddle out into the rain.

Chapter Two
The Enchanted Forest

Puddle bounded down the garden
path, sniffing at one puddle and then
another. He crouched down near a
big pool of water.

"Is this the right puddle?" Harry asked, jumping in with both feet. Muddy water splashed into the air and rained down on Harry, Ruby and Puddle.

"I guess not," Ruby said, wringing out her plaits.

Puddle rolled on the ground with his mouth open and tongue lolling from side to side. Ruby thought he looked like he was laughing.

"Very funny, Puddle," Harry said, as he cleaned his glasses. His glasses and Puddle's fur were dotted with muddy spots.

Ruby leaned down and whispered in Puddle's furry ear, "That was very naughty."

The puppy raced to the biggest puddle at the end of the path. He danced circles round it, so quickly that Ruby was dizzy just from watching him. At last he gave a bark, leapt into the puddle and disappeared.

I wonder where we'll go this time, Ruby thought, standing at the edge of the puddle. "Are you ready?" she asked Harry. She swung her arms back and rose on to her tiptoes.

"You go first," Harry said, and gave her a playful shove.

Ruby closed her eyes – and jumped!

***

When Ruby opened her eyes, she
had landed in what seemed to be
a shadowy forest. Puddle whined
nervously and snuggled closer to
her legs.

"Where's Harry?" Ruby asked Puddle, giving him a comforting pat on the head. "Maybe he didn't jump."

She spun in a slow circle. Harry was nowhere to be seen. "We can't go on an adventure without Harry," Ruby said.

She felt a tap on her shoulder, which made her jump. She whipped around. "Harry!" she squealed. Even though Ruby loved magic, this appearing and disappearing took a little getting used to.

"This doesn't look like a very colourful adventure," Harry said, as he tucked in his shirt. "It's dark here."

"Lots of adventures start in a spooky forest," Ruby said. As her eyes adjusted, she thought she could see twisted tree branches and thick thorns all around them. "At least, I think we're in a forest."

Puddle started to sniff. He immediately ducked behind Ruby's legs again.

"Ruby," Harry said, "did you see something move over there?"

Ruby squinted. She could just make out a tall shape moving towards them. It seemed to be hunched over, with tattered black wings. Ruby thought she could see long hair and what looked like a big crooked nose. Then the creature stopped. The dark figure raised what appeared to be a magic wand, and pointed it right at Ruby.

"I can see it," Ruby whispered to Harry, "and it can definitely see us."

Chapter Three
Harry Disappears

"Eeeeeeeeeek!" Ruby screamed, running towards Harry.

"Aaaaaaaaaaah!" Harry shouted, rushing towards Ruby.

"Wooooooooot!" Puddle barked, and ran around in circles.

The terrified cousins bumped right into each other. "Quick!" Ruby said. "Which way should we go?"

"Here, through these trees," Harry said as he tried to shove the branches out of his way. They didn't move, but somehow the whole forest seemed to wobble. Puddle growled at the trees that were blocking his path.

"We can't get out." Ruby pushed at the trees, but instead of rough bark she felt a smooth curtain. "Do you think that creature cast a spell?" Ruby asked.

"Maybe it's some kind of force field, like in a space movie," Harry suggested, crawling on his hands and knees to inspect the strange forest.

Ruby glanced back. "The creature is getting closer," she whispered.

But Harry didn't answer. He'd disappeared again!

Puddle barked and scrabbled at the ground with his paws. Ruby dropped to her knees and tried to find the spot where Harry had vanished. Puddle growled as the dark figure approached. Her heart pounding, Ruby found what seemed to be the bottom of the forest wall. She slid her hands under and lifted it up.

"It's like a magic trapdoor," she said, as she wriggled underneath. Puddle yelped and crawled after her.

Suddenly it was daylight. Ruby

blinked as Harry came into focus.
She looked behind her to see if the
strange creature had followed. But
now the forest had disappeared!
Ruby shook her head. It was all too
confusing! In place of the forest was
just a plain white curtain.

"Where are we?" Ruby asked

Harry, as he pulled her to her feet.

"I'm not sure, but we aren't alone,"
Harry said. A smiling girl was
staring at Ruby.

She was dressed in a leotard, tights and pink ballet shoes, complete with silky ribbons tied around her ankles. Her blonde hair was brushed back into a bun on the top of her head, except for one curl that hung down by the side of her face. She twisted it round her finger as she spoke. "Where did you come from?"

"We could ask you the same thing," Ruby said. She tried to smile, but her body was still buzzing from the fright of the shadowy forest and the scary creature.

"Something followed us here," Harry added. "I think we need to hide."

"See, Puddle agrees," Ruby said, as the puppy tugged at the silky ribbons on the girl's shoes, trying to pull her along but accidentally untying them.

"What on earth are you doing here?" said a cross voice from behind them.

"I think it's too late for hiding," the girl said with a gulp.

Chapter Four
The Magic of the Stage

A tall lady in a dark leotard and long skirt strode over. She frowned at Ruby, Harry and Puddle. "You've interrupted the final dress rehearsal for my ballet."

"Dress rehearsal?" Ruby said.

"Of course," Harry said, looking around. "We're in a theatre! This is the stage," he said, pointing at the wooden floorboards under their feet.

"But where's the forest?" Ruby asked, scratching her head.

"It's painted on the backdrop that you just crawled under," said the lady. "Look." She clapped her hands and gestured to someone at the side of the stage.

The plain backdrop next to them flew into the air. Puddle barked at the vanishing curtain. As they stood underneath it, they could see the twisted trees of the forest painted on the back of the curtain. There was another forest painted on a curtain at the back of the stage too.

The lady clapped again, and the

huge red velvet curtain at the front
of the stage opened. Ruby, Harry and
Puddle stared out in amazement at
the rows and rows of seats in front
of them.

"I am Miss Sue," the lady
continued. "And this is
Elizabeth." The
girl in the leotard
curtsied. "Would
you kindly tell
me who you
are and what you
are doing here?"
"I'm Ruby. This is
my cousin Harry,
and this is Puddle.
We were trying to
escape from a terrifying creature."

"You mean that creature?"
Elizabeth said, giggling as she
pointed behind them.

Ruby and Harry turned to see a slightly taller girl standing in the bright spotlights. She was wearing a green wig, a bumpy rubber nose and wings made of lace.

"I'm Kate," the girl said. "I'm only pretending to be a scary fairy. It's my part in the ballet."

Puddle galloped over and hopped into Kate's arms. He licked her face.

"I was never really scared," Harry said, but he looked relieved.

"The girls were just about to rehearse their dance for *Sleeping Beauty*," Miss Sue said. "You can watch from the wings, if you like."

"The wings," Ruby repeated, searching for feathers.

"That's what they call the sides of the stage that the audience can't see," Elizabeth said, taking her position with Kate on the stage.

Miss Sue signalled for the music to start as Ruby, Harry and Puddle rushed off-stage. They watched the girls twirl and whirl together. They sprang so high into the air it was as

if their feet were made of springs.
Puddle's tail wagged in time to
the music.

"Elizabeth looks just like a gazelle when she jumps. I wish I could dance like that," Ruby whispered to Harry. "Gazelle, gazelle, froggy jump, gazelle, gazelle, spinning top," she said quietly to herself.

"What are you doing?" Harry asked, leaning in close to Ruby.

"I'm memorizing Elizabeth's dance so I can do it when we get back home," Ruby replied. "Froggy jump, gazelle, spinning top, spinning top."

Puddle barked and hopped across the stage on his back legs.

"Look, Puddle's dancing too," Elizabeth said, laughing as the dance came to an end.

"Maybe Puddle will make his debut tonight as well," said Kate, nudging Elizabeth.

"Could I help make a 'debut'? I'm very good at making things," Ruby said.

"You make a 'debut' when you perform your first lead role in a show," explained Kate.

Miss Sue nodded. "And Elizabeth is making her debut today as the princess."

"Yes," said Elizabeth. "Later in the show I have to dance on the stage all by myself." There was a slight tremble in her voice and she twisted her curl of hair round and round her finger.

"I'm sure you'll be great, Elizabeth," Harry said, pushing his glasses back into place.

Miss Sue checked her watch. "My stars, look at the time. Please clear the stage, everyone. The audience will be here soon."

As Elizabeth looked out at the empty theatre, Ruby thought she spotted a tear in her eye. What could be wrong with the star of the show?

Chapter Five
Hidden Treasures

As Elizabeth walked off-stage
with Ruby, Harry and Puddle, she
whispered, "I've never performed
in front of a proper audience before.
What if I mess it up?"

"Lots of performers get stage
fright," Harry interrupted. "Try not
to worry about it."

"I know you're right," Elizabeth

said, wrapping her stray curl round her finger again. "But I can't help it."

"Excuse me!" They all stepped aside as a man dressed in black, carrying a giant painted nutcracker, hurried past. "Better get this out of the way." He headed towards the stairs at the back of the stage. Puddle raced after him.

"Wait, Puddle," Ruby called after the naughty puppy.

"Puddle's got the right idea," Elizabeth said, brightening. "Do you want to see the most amazing thing?"

Elizabeth, Ruby, Harry and Puddle followed the man down a

winding staircase. They stayed close
behind him as he snaked round the
theatre's basement. Harry had to
drag Ruby along because she wanted
to stop and look at everything.
They passed a clothes rail full of
pirate costumes with polished
brass buttons.

Round the corner
was a fluffy white object on a stand.

"What's that?" asked Ruby, pointing. "It looks like a powdered poodle."

Puddle hunched down and growled at the white furry thing.

Elizabeth giggled. "It's not a poodle – it's a wig."

Down another corridor Ruby saw a basket full of pink ballet shoes of all different sizes. She wondered if one of the pairs would fit her. She had always wanted a pair of proper ballet shoes.

Finally, the man went into a room with the word 'Props' painted on the door.

"What does 'Props' mean?" Ruby whispered.

"Property of the theatre," Harry said. "It's all the items that performers use on stage – like fake swords or magic wands."

After a moment, the man left the props room and walked away.

"Come on," said Elizabeth as she opened the door. Ruby thought the room smelled just like the arts and crafts cupboard at school.

"Look at all these things," Ruby said, wide-eyed.

Puddle barked as he bounded up to a large feather headdress and sniffed. He sneezed and rubbed his nose with his paws.

The room was crammed with swans' wings, fairy wands, Spanish fans and jewelled crowns. Puddle rushed around inspecting everything. There was an oversized wooden dollhouse in one corner and a large stuffed crocodile in the other. Harry noticed some rose bushes leaning against the wall.

"They look so real," he said, touching them. "Ouch! Right down to the thorns."

Ruby gazed up at a giant lollipop with yellow and red swirls. "I wish this was real," she said, imagining that the big lolly would taste like banana and strawberry.

"That's from *The Nutcracker* – one of my favourite ballets," Elizabeth said. "But this is my favourite thing in the entire props room." She pulled back a huge white dust sheet to reveal a pumpkin carriage on golden wheels.

"It's Cinderella's magic coach!" Ruby said, jumping up and down with excitement. "Can we go inside?"

"Of course," Elizabeth said.

Ruby and Elizabeth climbed
into the carriage while Harry and
Puddle sat at the front, pretending
to hold the reins of imaginary horses.
Ruby waved out of the window and
imagined she was Cinderella on her
way to the ball.

She was jolted from her daydream by a voice booming over the loudspeaker: "Miss Elizabeth to the dressing room, please."

"I've got to get ready," said Elizabeth, hurrying out of the pumpkin carriage.

Ruby and Harry draped the dust sheet back over it, careful to leave everything just as they had found it. They all raced out of the props room and down the corridor – until they came to another corridor that looked exactly the same.

"I can't remember which way we came," Harry said, scratching his head. "We just followed that man carrying the nutcracker. I wasn't paying that much attention."

Puddle paced up and down.

"It's a maze down here. We'll never get back in time for the show," Elizabeth said. "We're lost!"

Chapter Six
A Crazy Maze

"That's it," said Harry.

"That's it? You're giving up?" Ruby exclaimed.

"No – that's it! Elizabeth just said that it's a maze down here, and I'm good at mazes. I do them in my puzzle book all the time." Harry adjusted his glasses. "We can work this out. We just have to remember what we saw on the way in, and look for those things on the way out."

"Pirate clothes, poodle wigs . . . oh, what was next?" Ruby said.

Harry read a sign on the wall. It had arrows pointing in every direction. "Well, this way is a workshop, and down there is the shoe room," Harry said.

"I remember!" Ruby shouted. "Pirate clothes, poodle wigs and pretty princess pumps!"

Ruby, Harry, Elizabeth and Puddle walked quickly down the corridor. But they couldn't find the pirate clothes from Ruby's rhyme.

"This isn't the right way," Elizabeth said, twisting the stray curl round her finger.

"Wait a minute," said Harry. "We have to do the rhyme in reverse. It's not, 'Pirate clothes, poodle wigs and pretty princess pumps' – it's 'Princess pumps, poodle wigs and pirate clothes'."

"Harry, you're a genius!" Elizabeth exclaimed.

"And there are the ballet shoes!" Ruby cried, running down the corridor, past the overflowing baskets of pink ballet slippers.

"And there's the powdered wig that looks like a big white poodle," Elizabeth said as they turned the corner. They continued until they reached another turning point.

"There are the pirate clothes," Elizabeth said, clapping her hands. "We did it!"

Right at the end of the corridor was Miss Sue, standing by the dressing room door and tapping her watch. "My stars, Elizabeth. What's kept you?"

"Sorry," Elizabeth said as they filed into the dressing room.

Elizabeth stood, not moving, in front of the dressing room mirror while the other dancers got ready.

"You've got to get ready," Ruby said. She spotted the pole with

tutus stacked on top of each other.
She thought it looked like a baby's
stacking-rings toy. "Which one is
yours?"

Elizabeth pointed to a pretty blue
and yellow flowered tutu. Ruby held
it steady while Elizabeth stepped
into it. Elizabeth twisted her lock
of hair round her finger, faster and
faster.

"There's no need to be nervous
now," Harry said. "We made it in
time."

Ruby noticed that all the other
girls wore their hair in neat buns
that shimmered with glitter. She
smoothed back Elizabeth's hair and

clipped her over-twirled strand into place.

"Now for the finishing touch," Ruby said. She picked up the pot of glitter. Puddle scampered over to inspect it. The puppy took a big sniff and then sneezed a glittery burst all over Elizabeth, Ruby and Harry.

"Oops! We'll just have to be extra sparkly," Ruby said. Puddle sneezed another splash of sparkles.

"It's time, Elizabeth," said Miss Sue. "Ready?"

Elizabeth tagged along behind Miss Sue and the other dancers.

"Break a leg!" Harry called out after Elizabeth.

"Harry!" gasped Ruby. "What a horrible thing to say."

"People in the theatre say it to each other all the time. It means good luck," Harry explained.

Ruby giggled and tugged her plaits to give Elizabeth some extra luck.

Ruby, Harry and Puddle waited

until the dressing room was empty,
then they made their way to the
wings to watch. The velvety red
front curtain was shut, but Kate was
already on stage. Puddle raced on to
the stage and circled Kate.

"Woof! Woof!" He barked up at Ruby and Harry.

"Wait – Puddle's right. Something's wrong," Ruby said.

"Where's Elizabeth?" Harry asked. "This is the part of the ballet where she dances with Kate, isn't it?"

Miss Sue paced back and forth, looking for Elizabeth. She shook her head sadly, and Kate lifted her arms to start the dance.

"Oh, no," said Ruby. "Without Elizabeth, the ballet will be ruined!"

Chapter Seven
Spinning in the Spotlight

"Maybe the ballet won't be ruined after all," said Harry, nudging Ruby towards the stage.

Puddle barked and pulled at Ruby's tutu. Miss Sue walked up to Ruby. "The show must go on," she said, handing Ruby a pair of ballet shoes.

"But I can't dance in front of all

those people," Ruby said, peeking through the curtain at the audience.

"You love to dance," Harry said. "Now's your chance."

Ruby took a deep breath, kicked off her wellies, slipped on the ballet shoes and twirled on to the stage.

The red curtain opened and the audience clapped. Ruby remembered her names for Elizabeth's dance steps. "Gazelle, gazelle, froggy jump," she repeated to herself. "Gazelle, gazelle, spinning top."

Ruby couldn't believe it. She was dancing in a real ballet! Kate smiled at her as they both glided around the stage.

When Ruby performed her final swan move and gracefully slid into the splits, the crowd clapped and cheered. Ruby tried to take a picture of this moment in her mind. She wanted to remember all the smiling faces.

Ruby walked back into the wings and Miss Sue gave her a big smile, as if to say thank you. But before Ruby could smile back, ballerinas in white tutus rushed past her on to the stage, taking their positions for the next dance.

Puddle hopped on his back legs until Ruby leaned down so he could give her a big lick on the nose.

"You were great," Harry said. "But we have to find Elizabeth before her big solo!"

Ruby nodded. "Let's think! Where could she be?"

Puddle barked and headed for the stairs. "I bet he's right," Harry said. "Come on!" They ran after the puppy.

"Now, which way was it?" Harry asked.

"Pirate clothes, poodle wigs and pretty princess pumps!" they both sang out together, and ran all the way to the props room. Inside, Puddle trotted over to Cinderella's pumpkin carriage and pointed a paw. Ruby

noticed that the white dust sheet had been taken off.

"I think Elizabeth's inside," she said to Harry.

Ruby knocked gently on the carriage door. "Elizabeth? Are you in there?"

The door slowly opened and Elizabeth stepped out. Puddle rubbed against her legs. She leaned down to stroke his ear.

"I'm sorry. I can't do my solo," she said. "There are so many people in the audience. I'm scared."

"But Kate and all your friends are counting on you. You have to try," said Harry.

Elizabeth simply shook her head and started twisting her hair round her finger again.

"You were fine dancing when Harry and I were watching, weren't you?" said Ruby.

Elizabeth nodded.

"Then what if Harry and I are on stage and you just dance for us?" Ruby suggested.

"But how can we be on stage

without being seen by the audience?"
Harry asked. He leaned on the fake
rose bushes next to him. "Ouch!
These thorns hurt!"

"We can put the rose bushes at the
front of the stage and hide behind
them," Ruby said. "Now you see me!"
She ducked behind one of the bushes.
"Now you don't!"

"I guess I can try," Elizabeth said.

"Then let's go," Ruby said.

Harry and Ruby each grabbed one of the pretend rose bushes, and they hurried back up to the stage.

"You can do it," Ruby said, hugging Elizabeth.

Harry gave Elizabeth a big thumbs up. Puddle nudged her towards the other dancers. Elizabeth nodded and flitted to the centre of the stage.

Ruby, Harry and Puddle hid behind the rose bushes and slowly crept to the front of the stage amid a flurry of tutus. The other dancers circled around Elizabeth, then danced off to the sides of the stage.

The curtain opened. This was her big moment! But instead of beginning her dance, Elizabeth stood frozen to the spot, staring out at the audience.

"Oh, no," Ruby whispered to Harry. "She's too scared to dance!"

Chapter Eight
The Curtain Call

"We need to get Elizabeth to look at us, not the audience," Harry said.

Puddle hopped up on his back legs, just as he had done in the rehearsal. Only this time, he was hidden by the bushes. Ruby waved to Elizabeth and then pointed at Puddle, who was hopping in time to the music. The sight made Elizabeth smile, and she began to dance.

When she finished, cries of "Bravo!" echoed round the theatre. As the dancers took their bows, the audience tossed flowers on to the stage.

"It's raining roses," Ruby said. Puddle grabbed a single red rose in his mouth. He headed straight for Elizabeth and placed the rose at her feet.

"Thanks, Puddle." Elizabeth was grinning from ear to ear. She patted Puddle on the head and took another bow with the other dancers.

Miss Sue walked on to the stage and motioned for Harry and Ruby to join her. The cousins came out of hiding and faced the audience. Harry bowed. As Ruby curtsied, she slipped on the stage and ended up doing the splits. The crowd cheered.

"I couldn't have done it without your help," Elizabeth whispered to Ruby and Harry. "You two saved the show. Oh, and Puddle, of course!"

Just then, Puddle trotted over to the front curtain and started to pull it closed.

"I think Puddle's trying to tell us that it's time to go," Ruby said, as the velvety curtain swung shut.

Ruby and Harry dashed off-stage.
Ruby slipped off her ballet shoes.
She wished she could take them
with her, but she
pulled on her
wellies instead.
Puddle
began
to race
round
Harry and Ruby.
The world went fuzzy. Ruby felt as
if someone was tickling her all over.

"Goodbye," called Miss Sue,
Kate and Elizabeth. "Thanks for
everything!"

***

When Ruby opened her eyes, she and Harry were once again in Grandad's garden. She splashed in every puddle on the path to the cottage. She fluttered her arms like a butterfly. Spun like a top. Kicked like a kangaroo. And then swayed her arms in the air like a tree in the wind.

"What are you doing?" Harry asked, staring at Ruby over the top of his rain-splattered glasses.

"I'm making up a new dance for when I'm a world-famous ballerina," Ruby said with a bow.

"Just make sure you wipe your muddy feet before you go inside Grandad's cottage," Harry said, and demonstrated wiping his feet on the wet grass. "I call this move 'the charging bull'." He lowered his head and bolted towards the front door.

"I call that 'my crazy cousin'," Ruby muttered.

Harry stumbled over the welcome mat. "Hey, what's this?"

Ruby picked up the pink slippers with their long, silky ribbons.

"Proper ballet shoes!" she squealed. She recognized the muddy paw prints on the mat. "Thanks, Puddle!" she called into the rainy-day breeze. She tugged her plaits for luck and wished for more rain.

Can't wait to find out
what Puddle will do next?
Then read on! Here is the first
chapter from Puddle's fourth
adventure, Rainforest Hide
and Seek . . .

Rainforest
Hide and Seek

"I'm a water fairy!" Ruby cried, wrapping a damp strand of feathery pondweed around her head and sticking a pink water lily behind one ear. "And I can make myself invisible."

Her plaits bounced as she waved her fishing net like a magic wand.

Ruby's cousin Harry stared at her.

"I can still see you," he said, pushing his glasses up his nose. He lifted his fishing net out of Grandad's pond and peered into it. "I've caught something!" he exclaimed.

"Let me look." Ruby raced over to Harry and peered inside the bulging, dripping net. "It's just lots of pondweed and tiny bits of sticks and stone," she said.

But then the pondweed moved. A little green frog sitting among the leaves began to ribbet.

"Wow!" Ruby said. "He's the exact

same colour as the pondweed."

"It's called camouflage," Harry said. He flicked through his favourite wildlife book, which was lying open at the pond-life page. "Lots of creatures use it to blend in with their surroundings, so no one can see them."

"Like they're invisible," Ruby said, smiling.

Ruby and Harry carefully tipped the frog on to a lily pad.

Ruby's pondweed crown fell off as she lay on her tummy at the edge of the pond and watched the frog hop from leaf to leaf.

Two electric-blue dragonflies whizzed and hovered overhead. Then a series of ripples spread out across the water.

Plop, plop … plop, plop … plop.

Ruby's heart leapt with joy. Huge raindrops were plopping into the pond, bouncing off the lily pads. Water dripped from her plaits as she sat up. "Where's Puddle?" she asked.

Whenever it rained, their naughty puppy friend arrived, and they went on magical adventures.

On the far side of the pond, a clump of rushes rustled.

"Woof! Woof!" Puddle bounded out of the rushes towards Ruby and Harry, wagging his tail. Ruby and Harry's wellies were in his mouth.

"Hello, boy," Ruby said, patting Puddle all over. "Where are you taking us today?"

The little puppy trotted up the garden path, where the rain had already made large puddles.

Ruby held her breath. When Puddle was around, a rainy puddle could become the gateway to a new and exciting adventure.

Puddle stopped at the largest pool of water, ran round it, jumped in – and disappeared.

Ruby turned to Harry and shouted, "One, two, three, JUMP!"

And into the puddle they went.

***

To find out what happens next,
get your copy of RAINFOREST
HIDE AND SEEK today!

Puddle
the naughtiest puppy

Magic Carpet Ride

Join Puddle, Ruby and Harry
on their first exciting adventure!

Aziz wants to win
the magic carpet
race so he can be
granted a wish
by the beautiful
princess! Can Ruby,
Harry and Puddle
help Aziz to win?

Find out in MAGIC CARPET RIDE...

Puddle
the naughtiest puppy

Toyshop Trouble

Join Puddle, Ruby and Harry
on their next thrilling adventure!

This time Puddle's
magic takes them
to an amazing
toyshop. Professor
Toyjoy needs help
to win the big toy
competition!
Will Puddle be
able to save the day?

Find out in TOYSHOP TROUBLE...

Puddle
the naughtiest puppy

Rainforest
Hide and Seek

Have you ever wanted to see a rainforest?

Puddle uses his
magic to take Ruby
and Harry through
a puddle and into an
incredible animal
adventure. Things
keep going missing
in the rainforest –
can Puddle figure
out why?

Find out in RAINFOREST HIDE AND SEEK…

Dragon Dance

Join Puddle, Ruby and Harry on
their new adventure in Chinatown!

Li wants to make
his Grandad proud
by appearing in the
Chinese festival.
Can Puddle and the
children help him
to get Lucky the
dragon to dance?

Find out in DRAGON DANCE...

Puddle
the naughtiest puppy

Magic Mayhem

Ruby and Harry are amazed to find themselves in a medieval castle...

...when Puddle takes them on their latest adventure! They meet a magician's apprentice who is in deep trouble. He's lost his spell book. Can Puddle save the day?

Find out in MAGIC MAYHEM...

Walking a dog

Hi, it's Ruby and Harry again, just back from our latest magical journey with Puddle the puppy. That was great fun! Once again, it's time to learn something about real dogs and what they need to be healthy and happy.

Our friends from **Dogs Trust** will kindly help us in our 'doggy discovery journey'! They are the experts! They look after lots and lots of real dogs and puppies each year. In fact, **Dogs Trust** is the UK's largest dog charity and is working towards the day when all dogs can enjoy a happy life in a loving home.

This time we will find out all about why walking your dog is so important. Like all of us, dogs need exercise to keep them nice and healthy and to stop them getting bored!

Always remember, Puddle is a magical dog, while real dogs and puppies are living animals who need a lot of care, love and attention.

Tips for walking your dog:

- Always walk your dog with an adult, to stay safe.
- Make sure your dog always wears a collar and tag. This is the law! Then, if your dog goes missing and is found, it can be returned to you.
- Always keep your dog on a lead. This means it will be safe at all times.
- Make sure the adult always picks up the dog poop. This will keep our streets and parks nice and clean (and remember – this is the law too!).
- Remember, your dog needs at least two walks a day to stay fit and healthy, even if it is raining!

Congratulations – you now understand why it is so important to take dogs for walks.

We will see you next time, when **Dogs Trust** will tell us about a dog's needs.

Remember, "A dog is for life, not just for Christmas®"
We have 18 Rehoming Centres around the UK and Ireland. To find out more please go to:
www.dogstrust.org.uk
For more fun and games please go to:
www.learnwithdogs.co.uk

Spot the Puddle Difference!

Here are two pictures of Puddle and his friends.

Look at the first picture carefully, then look at the second. Can you spot six tricky differences?

Ruby's Ballet Mix-up

Ruby is trying to learn some graceful ballet moves, but she can't remember their names. Can you remember which moves Ruby learns? Unscramble the letters to find the words.

plists

sequebara

tirouptee

Answers on the next page

Answers to Puddle Puzzles:
Spot the Puddle Difference: Puddle has vanished, Ruby has flowers on her top, Ruby's tutu has more lines on it, Harry's welly has turned black, Elizabeth's foot has vanished, there is an extra line on the wall
Ruby's Ballet Mix-up: splits, arabesque, pirouette

For more magical adventures, come and play with Puddle at

www.puddlethepuppy.com

Use this special code to get extra-special games and free stuff at puddlethepuppy.com

BALLET
SHOES